# Erik and the Three Goats

Written by Gale Clifford

Illustrated by Diane Fiedler

Silver Burdett Ginn
A Division of Simon & Schuster
160 Gould Street
Needham Heights, MA 02194 - 2310

Modern Curriculum Press
A Division of Simon & Schuster
299 Jefferson Road, P.O. Box 480
Parsippany, NJ 07054 - 0480

Design and production by BIG BLUE DOT

ISBN: 0-663-59414-6  Silver Burdett Ginn
ISBN: 0-8136-0987-9  Modern Curriculum Press


1 2 3 4 5 6 7 8 9 10  SP  01 00 99 98 97 96 95

Once a boy named Erik had three goats. Each goat wore a blue collar and a blue bell. Every day the goats walked up the trail to eat grass. Every night they walked back down.

3

One day the three goats leaped across the trail. They leaped over a fence and began to chew the grain.

Erik could not get his goats to leave.
They chewed and chewed on the grain.
Erik sat down and began to cry.

Then along came a rabbit. "Why do you cry?" asked the rabbit.

"I cry because my goats won't leave," said Erik.

"I'll try to help," said the rabbit.

But the rabbit could not get the three
goats to leave.

The rabbit sat down with Erik and
began to cry, too.

Then along came a fox. "Why do you cry?" asked the fox.

"I cry because the boy cries," said the rabbit. "The boy cries because his goats won't leave."

"I'll try to get them out," said the fox.

But the fox could not get the three
goats to leave.

The fox sat down with Erik and the
rabbit and began to cry, too.

Then three bees flew by. "Why do you cry?" asked the bees.

"I cry because the rabbit cries," said the fox. "The rabbit cries because the boy cries. The boy cries because his goats won't leave."

"We'll help," said the bees.
"You?" they all said as they laughed.

The bees flew to the goats. "Buzz, buzz, buzz," they said. And the three goats leaped from the grain.